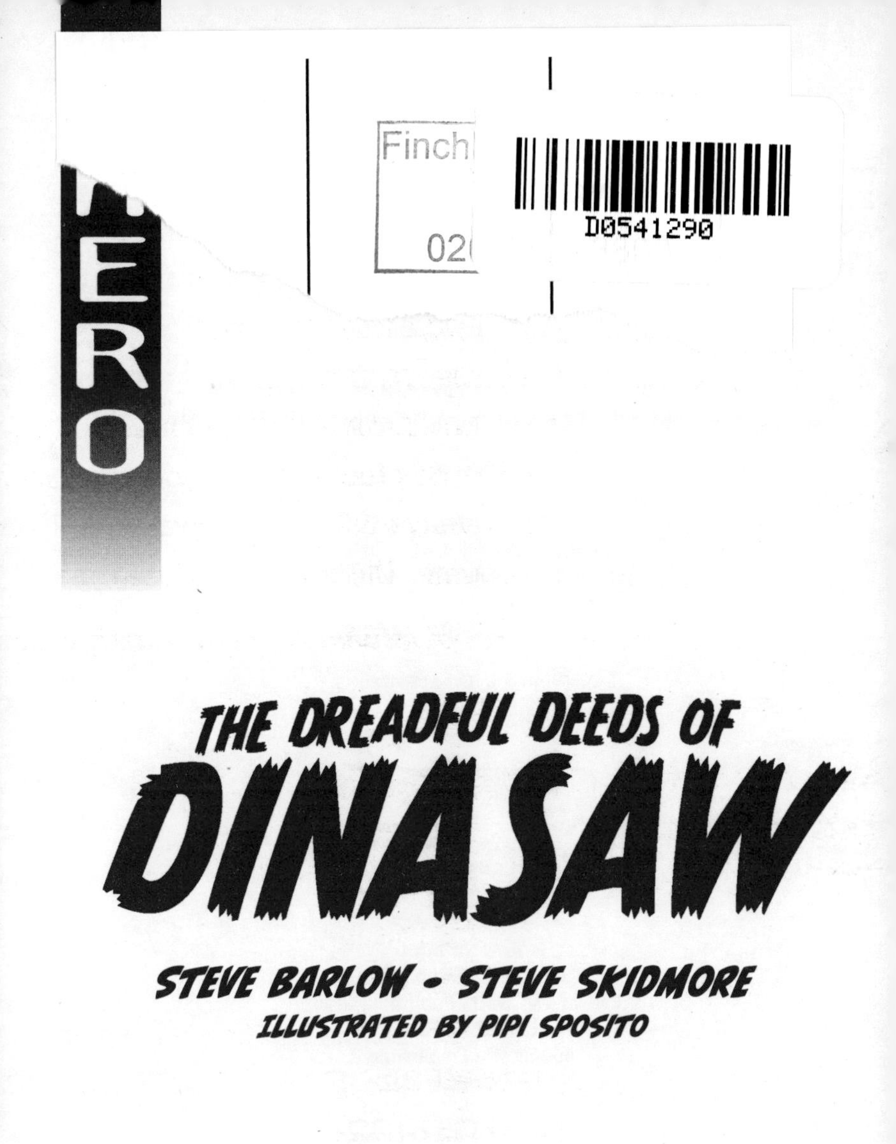

THE DREADFUL DEEDS OF DINASAW

STEVE BARLOW - STEVE SKIDMORE
ILLUSTRATED BY PIPI SPOSITO

Franklin Watts
First published in Great Britain in 2020
by The Watts Publishing Group

Design: Cathryn Gilbert

ISBN 978 1 4451 7008 4
ebook ISBN 978 1 4451 7006 0
Library ebook ISBN 978 1 4451 7007 7

1 3 5 7 9 10 8 6 4 2

Printed in Great Britain

Franklin Watts
An imprint of
Hachette Children's Group
Part of The Watts Publishing Group
Carmelite House
50 Victoria Embankment
London EC4Y 0DZ

An Hachette UK Company
www.hachette.co.uk

www.franklinwatts.co.uk

HOW TO BE A MEGAHERO

Some superheroes can read books with their X-ray vision without opening the covers or even when they're in a different room ...

Others can read them while flying through the air or stopping a runaway train.

But that stuff *IS* just small potatoes to you, because you're not a superhero. You're a ***MEGAHERO***!

YES, this book is about **YOU**! And you don't just read it to the end and then stop. You read a bit: then you make a choice that takes you to a different part of the book. You might jump from Section 3 to 47 or 28!

If you make a good choice, ***GREAT!***

BUUUUUUT ...

If you make the wrong choice ... **DA-DA-DAAAH!**

ALL KINDS OF BAD STUFF WILL HAPPEN.

Too bad! It's no good turning green and tearing your shirt off. You'll just have to start again. But that won't happen, will it?

Because you're not a zero, or even a superhero. You are ... ***MEGAHERO***!

You are a **BRILLIANT INVENTOR** – but one day **THE SUPER PARTICLE-ACCELERATING COSMIC RAY COLLIDER** you'd made out of old drinks cans, lawnmower parts and a mini black hole went critical and scrambled your molecules (nasty!). When you finally stopped screaming, smoking and bouncing off the walls, you found your body had changed! Now you can transform into any person, creature or object. **HOW AWESOME IS THAT?!!!**

You communicate with your ***MEGACOMPUTER*** companion, **PAL**, through your ***MEGASHADES*** sunglasses (which make you look pretty COOL, too). **PAL** controls the things you turn into and ***almost hardly ever crashes and has to be turned off and on again!*** This works perfectly – unless you have a bad WIFI signal, or **PAL** gets something wrong – but hey! That's computers for you, right?

Like all heroes, your job is to SAVE THE WORLD from **BADDIES AND THEIR EVIL SCHEMES**. But be back in time for supper. Even ***MEGAHEROES*** have to eat ...

Go to 1.

1

Following another successful mission, you are in a café in Washington DC checking the news on your ***MEGA CELLPHONE*** when a **BREAKING NEWS** story appears ...

A GIANT FLYING REPTILE APPARENTLY MADE OF SCRAPYARD JUNK, WHICH OBSERVERS HAVE INSTANTLY DUBBED THE TERROR-SOAR, HAS APPEARED IN THE SKIES ABOVE THE NATION'S CAPITAL.

To ignore the story, go to 14.

To investigate it, go to 33.

2

"Change me into a peregrine," you tell PAL.

Instantly you turn into a black and white bird with flippers.

"Not a **PENGUIN!**" you tell PAL. "A **PEREGRINE** falcon!"

PAL obeys.

You chase after the Terror-soar — but it flies into storm clouds and you lose it. Thunder splits the air, rain lashes down on you — and then a bolt of lightning strikes, sending you tumbling from the sky.

DA-DA-DAAAH!

That was bolt from the blue!

Go back to 1.

3

PAL accesses the files of the **INTERNATIONAL CYBERNETICS CORPORATION** to find out what turned brilliant scientist Dinah Shaw into unhinged supervillain DinaSaw.

"IT SEEMS THEY FIRED HER FOR INVENTING WEIRD STUFF LIKE CARNIVOROUS VACUUM CLEANERS AND FLAME-THROWING TOASTERS. THEN SHE MOVED TO ARIZONA."

"Why Arizona?"

"WELL, THIS IS JUST A GUESS – BUT YOU'VE SEEN THAT **TERROR-SOAR** SHE BUILT – IT MUST HAVE USED A LOT OF SCRAP. AND THE BIGGEST AIRCRAFT JUNKYARD IN THE WORLD IS IN ARIZONA."

To wait for DinaSaw's next move, go to 10.

To head for Arizona, go to 28.

4

You have a brilliant idea. "Make me a chameleon!" you order PAL.

You change colour until you blend perfectly into the background, and head for a dark corner.

Unfortunately, you are still crossing the floor when lots of guards wearing big boots pile into the vault, and fail to notice you ...

SPLAT!

DA-DA-DAAAH!

You can hide, but you can't run! **Go back to 1.**

5

The Terror-soar still has the small jet in its huge talons.

"THAT WAS DINAH SHAW SPEAKING," says PAL. "SHE'S A BRILLIANT CYBERNETICS ENGINEER. SHE DESIGNED SOME OF THE PARTS YOU USED TO MAKE ME!"

"That explains a lot," you mutter.

"SORRY, ROGER?"

"Never mind ..."

The Terror-soar's pilot butts into the conversation. "Get lost, ***MEGA-FOOL***. I am no longer Dinah Shaw – I am supervillain DinaSaw, and unless the US government pays me 10 billion dollars, I shall destroy Air Force Two!"

To promise DinaSaw what she wants, go to 41.

To tell her to get lost, go to 36.

6

PAL turns you into a robo-raptor. In the darkness, the others do not notice. But when the Stinkysaurus stops outside Fort Knox and you rush out with the other robo-raptors, you find DinaSaw watching you from the cockpit of a new robot dinosaur shaped like a triceratops with three rotating drills jutting from its head.

"Hello, ***MEGA–PEST***," she says.

You return to human form. "How did you spot me?"

"The other robo-raptors are green," she says. "You're blue."

Thanks, PAL, you think.

"Now you're here," DinaSaw continues, "see if you can stop my Tridrillertops!"

You stare as the Tridrillertops starts tunnelling towards Fort Knox.

To stay in human form, go to 40.

To change into something else, go to 49.

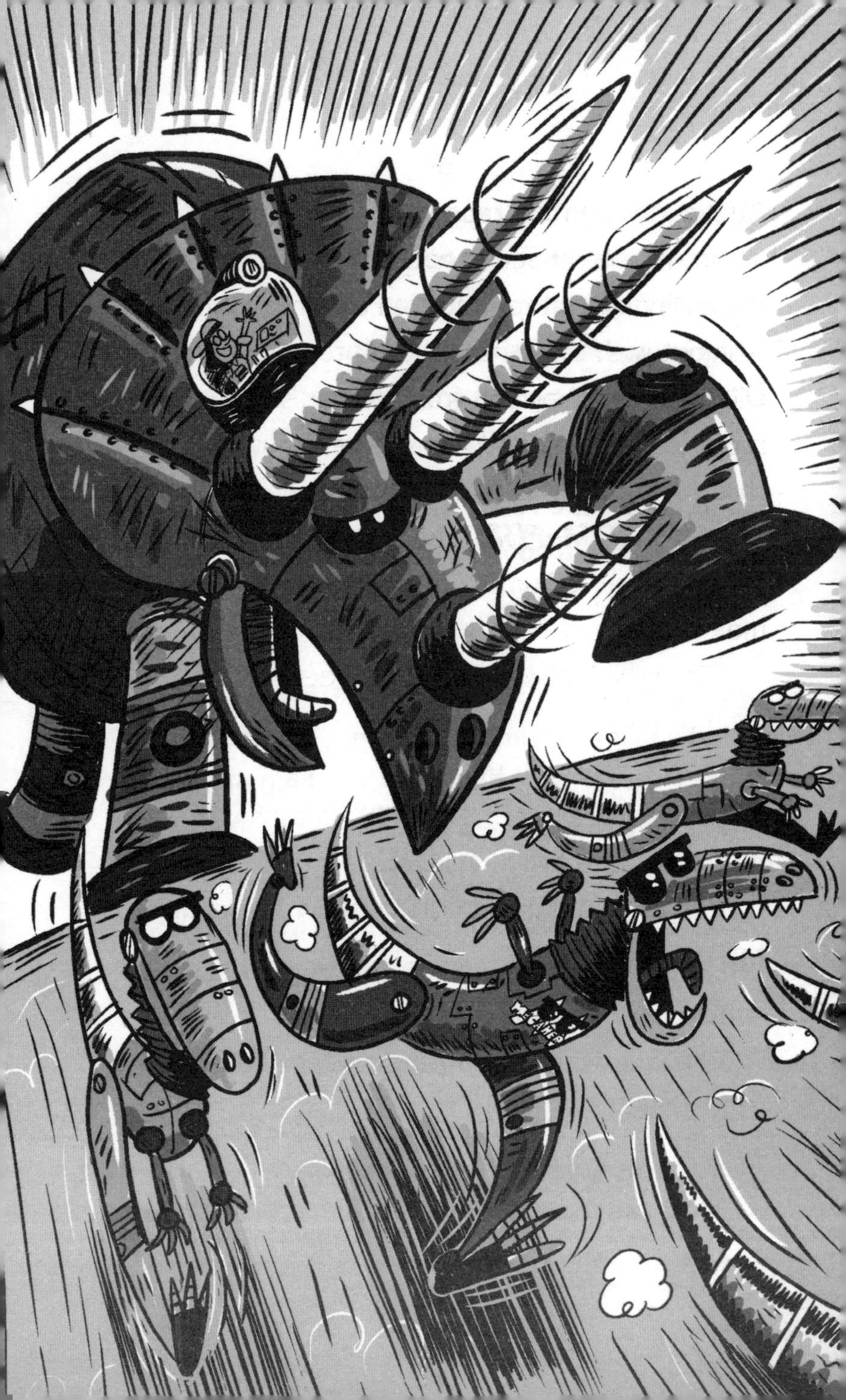

7

You chase the robo-raptors over the brow of a hill, in time to see them climbing aboard a caterpillar-tracked robot in the shape of a stegosaurus.

On the road behind you, you can see an armoured column of troops approaching.

To follow the robo-raptors, go to 34.

To call the troops for help, go to 18.

8

Guards rush into the vault and arrest you. It takes you a long time to convince them that you were trying to stop DinaSaw, not help her, but eventually they let you go.

"I'M PICKING UP ANOTHER NEWSFLASH," announces PAL. "IT'S **DINASAW** AGAIN – SHE'S GOT A NEW DINOSAUR ROBOT, AND SHE'S ATTACKING THE **UNIWORLD** THEME PARK AND DEMANDING A HUGE RANSOM TO STOP."

The guards offer to fly you to the UNIWORLD theme park.

To refuse, go to 24.

To accept, go to 38.

ALERT

9

As the *Stinkysaurus* lurches into motion, you hear a roaring sound above the engine and see a fiery glow appear. Robo-raptors start taking gold bars towards the glow. One picks you up and follows. Too late, you realise that they are melting the gold down in an electric furnace.

There is no time for you to react.

DA-DA-DAAAH!

The heat is on! *Go back to 1.*

10

Suddenly, the signal from PAL glitches.

"What's the matter?" you demand.

"THE **MEGACAVE** IS UNDER ATTACK ..."

The signal goes dead – you have lost PAL! Without the computer's vast database to help you, it will take you hours to change into something else – and while you dither, the Terror-soar reappears and swoops down on you, talons reaching out to snatch and tear ...

DA-DA-DAAAH! **The Terror-soar has settled your score. *Go back to 1.***

11

You land between the dinosaur and the convoy and turn into a giant concrete barrier.

The robot ankylosaurus simply smashes through you with its clubbed tail.

BANG, CRASH, WALLOP!

DA-DA-DAAAH!

You've gone to pieces! Pull yourself together and *Go back to 1.*

12

"Look at these poor people." You point at the petrified park punters. "They're terrified. Can't you see that what you're doing to them is wrong?"

DinaSaw cackles. "I make gigantic robotic killing machines. Do you think I care about people's feelings?"

The D. rex looms over you, raising one gigantic steel foot to stamp you into jelly.

DA-DA-DAAAH!

She has a point! ***Go back to 1.***

13

"Turn me into a rook," you tell PAL.

You become a chess piece like a small tower.

"Not that sort of rook – oh, never mind. Make me an owl."

PAL obeys.

You fly over rows of parked aeroplanes, many of them half-dismantled. Your night vision is excellent, but you can't see anything moving. Then you spot flashes of blue-white light, and head towards them ... nearer and nearer ...

To stay as an owl, go to 43.

To become something smaller, go to 23.

14

"AREN'T YOU GOING TO INVESTIGATE THIS **TERROR-SOAR**?" asks PAL.

You slurp your coffee. "No, it's probably just an Unidentified Flying Dinosaur or something."

At this point, an air-to-surface missile hits the café, which blows up around you.

You look up through the hole where the roof used to be. "Maybe I'd better investigate after all ..."

Go to 33.

15

You look around, searching for anything that might give you a clue about DinaSaw's plans.

You find an untidy office in a nearby hangar. There is a road map pinned to a board, showing the route from New York to a location in Kentucky, with a circle drawn on it in felt tip ... but what does it mean?

To wait for news of what DinaSaw is up to, go to 25.

To go to the location marked on the map, go to 32.

16

You turn into a small flying mammal.

"Not a **BAT**," you hiss to PAL, "a **BLACK CAT**."

You become flat and absorbent, like a thick towel.

"That's a **BATH-MAT**! I want to be a tomcat."

You turn into a tall item of headgear.

"Not a **TOP HAT**! A **TOMCAT**!"

"WELL, STOP WHISPERING – I CAN'T HEAR YOU." PAL turns you into a cat.

"I have to whisper or she'll hear ..."

"Who's that whispering?" DinaSaw appears, carrying a sack. "Aha – ***MEGAHERO***. Time for you to scat!" She pounces.

DA-DA-DAAAH!

You've let the cat out of the bag! ***Go back to 1.***

17

You fly at the Terror-soar, lashing out with your powerful claws, and it lets go of Air Force Two to fight you.

"SHOULDN'T YOU BE HELPING THE POOR PASSENGERS IN THAT AEROPLANE IT WAS ATTACKING, ROGER?" asks PAL.

"Don't call me Roger!" You break off the fight and speed down to the plane. Using your ***MEGA*** strength, you pull the plane out of its dive and land it on the ground.

However, the Terror-soar has followed you. It sneaks up on you, grips you in its claws and squeezes and squeezes ...

DA-DA-DAAAH!

Looks like you're short of breath! ***Go back to 1.***

18

You race towards the troops, waving frantically towards DinaSaw's robot stegosaurus.

"They're getting away!" you cry. "STOP THEM!"

The troops obey and open fire – but the dinosaur shoots out shells of knockout gas. The soldiers fall unconscious, and so do you.

By the time you come round, DinaSaw has escaped with the gold.

You're out for the count! *Go back to 1.*

19

You turn into a bull elephant and charge the D. rex.

But even the biggest elephants only weigh around 6,000 kilograms. The D. rex weighs twice that, and it's made of metal. You fall back, dazed and helpless.

The D. rex pounces, jaws closing around your neck ...

DA-DA-DAAAH!

Pack your trunk and *Go back to 1.*

MEGAHERO

20

You swoop down on the plane and reach out to grab it. "Turn me into the Roc!" you tell PAL.

Immediately, you become a huge limestone boulder.

"Not a **ROCK**!" you yell. "**THE ROC**! No '**K**'. The legendary giant bird that can carry an elephant!"

"I DON'T THINK I HAVE ONE IN MY DATABASE," SAYS PAL. "WOULD A PIGEON DO?"

It's too late. The plane is about to hit the ground – and so are you.

DA-DA-DAAAH!

You're stuck between a rock and a hard place. ***Go back to 1.***

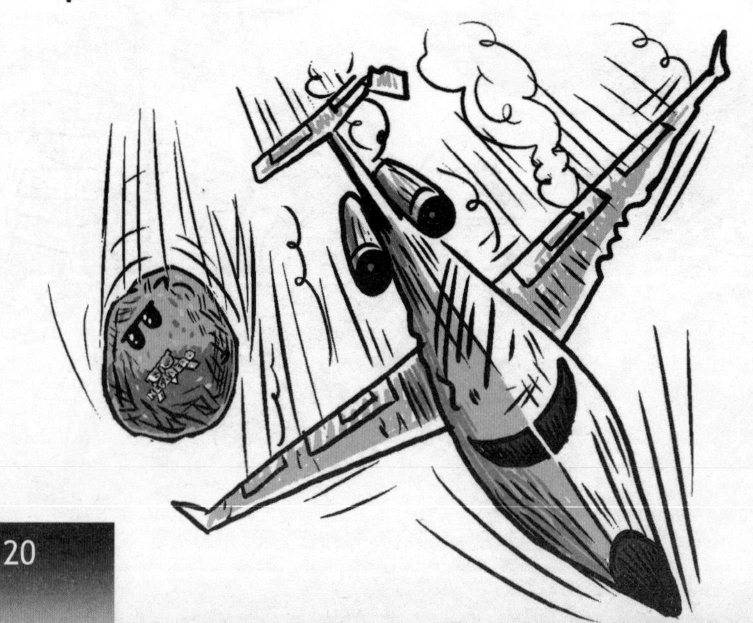

21

PAL turns you into a garden maze. The robo-raptors wander about between your high hedges, lost and confused.

"Very clever, ***MEGADODO,***" snarls DinaSaw, "but that won't hold me up for long!"

The Angryosaurus trundles up and bashes your maze to bits with its tail. You return to human form nursing a terrible tummy-ache. The Angryosaurus has come to a halt, apparently abandoned, and the robo-raptors hurry away with their armfuls of gold.

To follow the robo-raptors, go to 7.

To try and stop them, go to 39.

22

You ask PAL to turn you into a squirrel.

"YOU'RE PLANNING TO CHEW THROUGH SOME WIRES?" guesses PAL. "GOOD IDEA!"

You squeeze in between plates behind the Tridrillertops's armoured neck and burrow your way into its control centre. You find a multicoloured cable that looks important.

To unplug the cable, go to 42.

To nibble through it, go to 46.

23

You ask PAL to turn you into a cockroach. On the downside, you're not very fast now and you're too low down to see much, but you are small enough to get close to DinaSaw's secret workshop without triggering any security systems.

DinaSaw is welding together bits of aircraft junk, but your cockroach vision isn't good enough to see what she's making.

To change into a cat, go to 16.

To become human and arrest DinaSaw, go to 31.

24

"No thanks," you say. "I'm fed up of being chased around by junko-sauruses. I'm going to make myself into one of the biggest dinosaurs that ever was – then let's see them bully me!"

PAL turns you into a diplodocus. You are now very big and very strong – but also very slow. You've barely walked a couple of miles before PAL reports that the UNIWORLD theme park has been flattened – it's a disaster!

DA-DA-DAAAH!

A diplodocus has a brain the size of a walnut, but it's still bigger than yours! ***Go back to 1.***

25

You mooch around the aircraft boneyard for hours, waiting for news.

"I'VE GOT SOMETHING," says PAL. "THOUSANDS OF GOLD BARS HAVE BEEN STOLEN FROM FORT KNOX BY GIANT ROBOTS CONTROLLED BY **DINASAW**."

You feel a chill in your stomach. Fort Knox is almost 2,000 miles away. You'll never get there in time. DinaSaw has beaten you.

A *MEGAHERO* doesn't hang around! *Go back to 1.*

26

"Maybe that thing has a pilot," you say. "Let me talk to it."

PAL opens a radio link to the Terror-soar.

"This is ***MEGAHERO***," you say. "Call off your attack."

"FOOL!" snarls a female voice. "**YOUR FEEBLE POWERS ARE NO MATCH FOR MY TERROR-SOAR!**"

"I KNOW THAT VOICE," says PAL.

To attack the Terror-soar, go to 17.

To keep the pilot talking, go to 5.

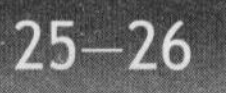

MEGAHERO

27

You take a step towards the robot T. rex and raise a hand.

"DinaSaw, stop! What are you hoping to get from this?"

"**REVENGE!**" snarls the deranged dinosaur fan. "You stopped me robbing the gold convoy and cleaning out the vault at Fort Knox – but you'll never beat my D. rex!"

"Shouldn't that be T. rex?"

"It's my dinosaur, it's named after me!"

To reason with DinaSaw, go to 12.

To trap the D. rex, go to 35.

To fight it, go to 19.

28

PAL turns you into a fast military jet, and you fly towards Arizona. Night is falling as you land at a **USAF** base near to the aircraft junkyard.

You have to decide on the best form to take to try and discover what DinaSaw is up to.

To turn into a bird, go to 13.

To turn into an animal, go to 37.

MEGAHERO

29

You turn into a zorb ball and surround one of the robo-raptors. It bounces around inside you, helpless; but the other robo-raptors come to its aid. You're about to be popped!

DA-DA-DAAAH!

The robo-raptors could see right through you! *Go back to 1.*

Go back to 1.

"I'm going down!" you tell PAL. "Radio the plane. Tell the passengers to jump out!"

"ROGER, ROGER."

You dive for the ground, where you immediately order PAL to turn you into a huge trampoline. Much to your relief, the passengers on the plane obey your order and jump for their lives. The stricken jet crashes, but the passengers hit you and bounce.

You return to human form to receive the president's thanks. As he and his staff stagger unsteadily away, you tell PAL, "I don't think we've seen the last of DinaSaw ..."

Go to 3.

31

You turn to human form. "DinaSaw! You will pay for your crimes!"

DinaSaw swings round and glares. "Oh, no, ***MEGAHERO***! The people at **INTERNATIONAL CYBERNETICS** who sacked me for no reason, and all their stooges in government – they'll pay!"

She takes a smartphone from her pocket and stabs at its screen. Piles of what look like junk turn into horrific half-finished robots and attack you. By the time you have fought them off, DinaSaw is nowhere to be seen.

In the distance, you spot the Terror-soar taking off.

To follow the Terror-soar, go to 2.

To look around, go to 15.

32

You turn into a fast military helicopter and fly through the night, setting your own autopilot so you can get some sleep.

At dawn next day, you arrive at the spot shown on the map in DinaSaw's office. You see a line of trucks below.

"THOSE TRUCKS," says PAL, "ARE TRANSFERRING SQUILLIONS OF DOLLARS' WORTH OF GOLD BARS FROM THE FEDERAL RESERVE TO THE US BULLION DEPOSITORY AT FORT KNOX."

"How do you know that?" you ask.

"IT WAS ON TWITTER."

You spot a gigantic robot dinosaur with a clubbed tail like an ankylosaurus, heading for the convoy.

To attack the dinosaur, go to 48.

To defend the convoy, go to 11.

33

"Turn me into an eagle," you tell PAL.

You become a hunting dog with floppy ears.

"That's a **BEAGLE**," you say.

"OH, SORRY."

PAL gets it right on the second try and you take flight.

"**TERROR-SOAR** AT TEN O'CLOCK," reports PAL.

"But it's already half past four."

"I MEAN IT'S HIGH UP AND TO YOUR LEFT."

You spot the Terror-soar. It looks like a gigantic steel robot copy of a pterodactyl. As you watch, it swoops down to attack a small jet aircraft. PAL picks up a distress call.

"**MAYDAY — THIS IS AIR FORCE TWO.**"

"What's Air Force Two?" you ask PAL.

"IT'S THE PLANE THEY USE WHEN AIR FORCE ONE WON'T START."

You gulp. "You mean, the President of the United States of America is on board?"

"YUP."

"I may need to fight the Terror-soar," you tell PAL. "You'd better turn me into a pterodactyl."

"ROGER."

"Does that mean 'yes'?"

"NO, IT'S WHAT I'M GOING TO CALL YOU – IT'S A GOOD NAME FOR A PTERODACTYL." PAL makes the change. "THERE YOU GO, ROGER."

To fight off the Terror-soar, go to 47.

To try to contact it, go to 26.

34

You sneak towards the line of hurrying robo-raptors and change into a gold bar. The first robot to come across this picks you up, thinking that one of the others must have dropped a bar from their load.

By now, US army troops have arrived and started shooting. DinaSaw mocks them.

“Pathetic! Do you think your feeble bullets can damage my Stinkysaurus?”

Why “Stinkysaurus”? you wonder. As if in reply, the waiting robot belches out ghastly gases from its rear end and fires teargas shells. The soldiers grasp at their throats and fall unconscious.

The robo-raptors aren’t affected – and neither are the gold bars. You are carried aboard the Stinkysaurus, which starts up and moves away.

To turn into a robo-raptor, go to 6.

To remain as a gold bar, go to 9.

35

You dance about in front of the D. rex, sticking your tongue out and waggling your fingers beside your ears. "Big bully! You don't scare me!"

"We'll see about that!" DinaSaw sends the D. rex lumbering towards you at a clanking run.

At the last possible moment, you change into a pit of hot, liquid tar. The D. rex can't stop in time. It blunders into the sticky goo and starts to sink.

Go to 50.

MEGAHERO

36

"You'll never get ten billion dollars," you sneer.

"Then I don't need this plane!" snarls DinaSaw. "Catch it if you can!"

The Terror-soar's powerful talons open and let the plane go.

To save the plane, go to 20.

To save the passengers, go to 30.

37

"I'll be a leopard," you tell PAL.

You change into the sort of stretchy bodystocking that dancers and wrestlers wear.

"Not a **LEOTARD**!" you snap. "A **LEOPARD**!"

"BE FAIR – I WAS ONLY ONE LETTER OUT!"

A leopard sees well in the dark. You prowl around until you spot blue-white flashes of light nearby. You creep closer for a better view ...

To change to something smaller, go to 23.

To stay as a leopard, go to 45.

38

The guards send you off in a Bell V-280 Valor tilt-rotor assault helicopter.

Approaching the UNIWORLD theme park, you see a robotic T. rex rampaging between the rides. Spotting you, it raises its arms, and fires a salvo of **SAM** missiles from its armpits. The helicopter is hit!

The pilot bails out and floats away on his parachute. You turn into a feather and waft gently to the ground, where you resume human form.

You find yourself surrounded by a panicking crowd – and a giant robotic T. rex is lumbering towards you!

To challenge DinaSaw, go to 27.

To run away, go to 44.

39

You order PAL to turn you into a gorilla – but you become a cute, fluffy South American rodent instead.

"I said a **GORILLA**," you rage, "not a **CHINCHILLA**!"

"OOPS ..." PAL makes another change.

As a giant silverback gorilla, you have the strength to throw robo-raptors about, putting them out of action. But there are too many of them and you are soon overpowered. The surviving robo-raptors hold you as the Angryosaurus arrives, lashing its terrible tail. You're about to be pounded to a pulp.

DA-DA-DAAAH!

Stop monkeying around. ***Go back to 1.***

40

You follow the Tridrillertops down the tunnel it is making, but you cannot run quickly over the chewed-up rocks and earth it leaves behind.

Then you hear a tortured groaning noise – and the tunnel collapses on top of you!

DA-DA-DAAAH!

That's a weighty problem! *Go back to 1.*

41

"Ten billion dollars," you say soothingly. "Sure, no problem ..."

Another voice breaks in. "This is ground control. The government refuses to release ten billion dollars to you at this time ..."

With a shriek of rage, the Terror-soar hurls the plane towards the ground.

To save the plane, go to 20.

To save the passengers, go to 30.

42

Finding the connector that plugs the cable into the Tridrillertops's electronic brain, you try to pull it out. This is hard work for your little squirrel paws, but eventually you succeed.

The Tridrillertops shuts down. You squeeze outside and find that the robo-raptors have also stopped working. You return to human form and make for the machine's cockpit – but it is empty. DinaSaw has escaped!

You hear the clattering footsteps of guards ...

To hide, go to 4.

To surrender, go to 8.

43

Suddenly, searchlights stab out of the darkness, blinding you.

"IDIOT!" cries DinaSaw's amplified voice. "Did you think I wouldn't have motion sensors to warn me you were coming? Bye, bye, birdie!"

Automatic machine-gun nests open fire. You are flying into a deadly hail of bullets!

DA-DA-DAAAH!

That put the "***OW***" in "***OWL***"! ***Go back to 1.***

44

You join the crowds racing for cover.

"PAL," you cry, "make me a greyhound!"

You turn into a big six-wheeled coach.

"Not a Greyhound bus!" you yell. "I meant the dog ..."

It's too late. The robot T. rex knocks you over with its tail and stomps you to smithereens.

DA-DA-DAAAH!

You're BUS-ted! ***Go back to 1.***

45

Suddenly, floodlights snap on. You freeze in the sudden glare.

"FOOL!" gloats DinaSaw's amplified voice. "My infrared sensors picked up your body heat!"

There is a mechanical clicking from all sides. You realise that you are surrounded by fierce-looking robots.

"Meet my robo-raptors," cackles DinaSaw.

The robo-raptors close in. There is no escape.

DA-DA-DAAAH!

Leopard, you've been spotted! *Go back to 1.*

46

You get your razor-sharp teeth to work on the cable's insulation. Something at the back of your nutty squirrel mind is just beginning to wonder whether this is really a good idea, when ...

That was the main power line!

DA-DA-DAAAH!

How shocking! ***Go back to 1.***

47

You climb towards the Terror-soar. It loosens its grip on the badly-damaged jet as it prepares to defend itself.

To continue the attack, go to 17.

To contact the Terror-soar, go to 26.

48

You turn into a rhino — but even a rhino charge isn't enough to stop the robot marauder. You stagger back with a headache.

PAL relays DinaSaw's mocking voice. "***MEGAHERO***! How d'you like my Angryosaurus?"

The gigantic robot starts smashing open the trucks of the convoy with its tail. Guards fire at it, but to no effect. Smaller robots with short arms and long legs appear, taking gold bars from the wrecked trucks.

"Take every last lovely bar, my robo-raptors!" gloats DinaSaw.

To fight the robo-raptors, go to 39.

To try and confuse them, go to 21.

49

"Make me a bat!" you tell PAL. You turn into a small buzzing insect.

"Not a **GNAT**! A **BAT**!"

"WELL, MAKE YOUR MIND UP ..."

You fly down the tunnel the Tridrillertops has made, hearing it collapse behind you. When you catch up with DinaSaw's machine, it has tunnelled into the vaults of Fort Knox and robo-raptors are loading it with gold.

To immobilise the Tridrillertops, go to 22.

To stop the robo-raptors, go to 29.

50

Helicopters arrive. One rescues the furious DinaSaw from the cockpit of the stranded D. rex.

Becoming human again, you are surrounded by relieved adults and disappointed kids. You realise that the D. rex has wrecked most of the theme park's rides.

No problem! You have PAL turn you into a super-scary pendulum ride! Soon, you are giving excited kids the time of their lives or (judging by their screams) the heebie-jeebies.

PAL is soon impatient. "HAVE YOU FINISHED FOOLING AROUND NOW?"

"No way!" you reply. "This is the most fun I've had in ages! Even ***MEGAHEROES*** need a day off every now and then!"

The End!

MEGAHERO

I HERO
MEGAHERO
LOOT
THE TERRIBLE TRICKS OF
MISS TAKE
Steve Barlow · Steve Skidmore
Illustrated by Pipi Sposito
EDGE

1

You are at the **GALACTIC COMICS CONVENTION**, signing autographs for your many fans. As you admire the top exhibit at the convention – a priceless, mint-condition copy of the first ever *Superduperman* comic – six ray-gun-toting "**ALIENS**" appear.

The audience applauds, thinking that this is all part of the show. But the applause turns to screams as the "**ALIENS**" spray gas from their "**RAY GUNS**". Panic-stricken fans stampede for the exits.

To tackle the "ALIENS", go to 18.

To change into a giant electric fan, go to 27.

CONTINUE THE ADVENTURE IN:

THE TERRIBLE TRICKS OF MISS TAKE

About the 2Steves

"The 2Steves" are Britain's most popular writing double act for young people, specialising in comedy and adventure. They perform regularly in schools and libraries, and at festivals, taking the power of words and story to audiences of all ages.

Together they have written many books, including the *I HERO Immortals* and *iHorror series*.

About the illustrator:

Pipi Sposito

Pipi was born in Buenos Aires in the fabulous 60's and has always drawn. As a little child, he used to make modelling clay figures, too. At the age of 19 he found out he could earn a living by drawing. He now develops cartoons and children's illustrations in different artistic styles, and also 3D figures, puppets and caricatures. Pipi always listens to music when he works.

Have you completed these I HERO adventures?

I HERO Immortals – more to enjoy!

978 1 4451 6963 7 pb
978 1 4451 6964 4 ebook

978 1 4451 6969 9 pb
978 1 4451 6971 2 ebook

978 1 4451 6957 6 pb
978 1 4451 6959 0 ebook

978 1 4451 6954 5 pb
978 1 4451 6955 2 ebook

978 1 4451 6960 6 pb
978 1 4451 6962 0 ebook

978 1 4451 6966 8 pb
978 1 4451 6967 5 ebook

Defeat all the baddies in Toons:

978 1 4451 5930 0 pb
978 1 4451 5931 7 ebook

978 1 4451 5921 8 pb
978 1 4451 5922 5 ebook

978 1 4451 5924 9 pb
978 1 4451 5925 6 ebook

978 1 4451 5918 8 pb
978 1 4451 5919 5 ebook

Also by the 2Steves...

978 1 4451 5985 0 hb
978 1 4451 5986 7 pb

978 1 4451 5976 8 hb
978 14451 5977 5 pb

978 1 4451 5982 9 hb
978 1 4451 5983 6 pb

978 1 4451 5972 0 hb
978 1 4451 5971 3 pb

978 1 4451 5892 1 hb
978 1 4451 5891 4 pb

978 1 4451 5988 1 hb
9781 4451 5989 8 pb

978 1 4451 5973 7 hb
978 1 4451 5974 4 pb

978 1 4451 5979 9 hb
978 1 4451 5980 5 pb